Bound
for
Release

Bound for Release

for

HONEY POT COLLECTION

Ali Whippe

4 Horsemen Publications, Inc.
1497 Main St. Suite 169
Dunedin, FL 34698
4horsemenpublications.com
info@4horsemenpublications.com

Cover & Typesetting by Battle Goddess Productions
Editor Nita Edetor

Print ISBN: 978-1-64450-138-2
Ebook ISBN: 978-1-64450-137-5

Dedication

For all the boys I've topped before

Chapter One

 aryBell knows what James wants the moment she lays eyes on him. It is easy enough to see. A tall man, broad-shouldered with short black hair and those wire-rimmed glasses that remind her of John Lennon even after Harry Potter got a hold of them, James slowly makes his way over to her table. She knows the type: alone at a fetish event—but not in that creepy stalker way some of the attendees cultivate—rather, a not-quite-vanilla curious to explore some part of himself that wants something more. His will be a serious interest, not a passing thing, not a bet or a joke.

Looking over the array of strap-ons, dildos, and phallic objects on her table, MaryBell knows that her wares are often the victim of snickered hilarity, visitors jostling one another with wide eyes and goofy grins: "Hey, dude, I bet you could fit this up your ass!" and the quick retort, "You would know!" Such banter is common at the bigger conventions. She sets up her table under the harsh fluorescent lights of the vendor room and spends the day balanced between serious members of the community looking for new toys to add to their collections and curious onlookers who dare one another to go into the room and look at "those freaky toys"—and that is fine. MaryBell loves her work, loves being "that girl" at conventions, the one who can match wits over teasing jests just as easily as she can sit down and discuss the merits of one style of strap-on versus another. MaryBell knows her trade, knows it well, and she is always glad to have some fun, but she really likes when someone comes along who is genuinely interested in what she has to offer, someone who wants to try something new, but doesn't know where to begin.

Someone like James.

She is suddenly glad that she agreed to this gig tonight, knowing that the smaller venue and limited audience at the Fetish Night/Dungeon Party at the Honey Pot instead of a local hotel means fewer people. The entrance fee for the event discourages the merely curious, allowing the well-versed members to have some fun in the dungeon set up nearby. MaryBell knows that her toys are harder to see in the relatively dim lighting, but the atmosphere encourages the attendees to act out scenes. To encourage them, the Honey Pot has a wide selection of BDSM equipment set up: spanking benches, St. Andrew's crosses, even a large metal cage large enough for a person to fit inside, hands bound to various points either above the head or at the waist. MaryBell hears the heavy thud of a leather paddle hitting flesh, and someone yelps and then moans. There are rules for playing at the event: no nudity, and no sex, but patrons are always happy to tie one another up and play with their toys—some brought from home and some purchased at the event.

It has been a good night, despite the smaller venue, but now that it is after midnight, things are winding down. Maybe after she packs up for the night in an hour or two, she might make her way over that way to the playroom. A few regulars tend to linger at the end of an event willing to perform one last scene. MaryBell doesn't think she will participate tonight, but she is always up for a bit of voyeurism.

Like watching the man who approaches her table now.

MaryBell lets her eyes linger on him as he walks up, taking in the details of his appearance in the dim light. He wears a green army jacket over a black t-shirt form fitting enough to see that he is in shape, but baggy enough to leave something to the imagination, and his jeans look comfortably worn. MaryBell decides she likes him. She doesn't move over to where he is though, knowing that someone with a serious interest will need time and space to take in the objects on her table on his own terms. When he is ready, he will come to her with his questions. She is content to wait, making a point to stand a little bit straighter though, improving her posture to accentuate her figure, just in case he cares to notice. She doesn't think he is gay, but sometimes she misreads these things.

James smiles briefly at her when he reaches the table, face open and friendly, not shy or embarrassed the way some patrons address her. She returns the look, but says nothing, watching as his eyes rove over the rows of plastic, rubber, hardwood, vinyl, and glass. He reaches out a curious hand to touch one of the glass dildos, fingers gently caressing the smooth surface, eyes creasing in surprised delight.

"It's a different sensation," MaryBell offers in a neutral tone, allowing him to decide if he wants to engage in conversation or just nod and move on.

"I imagine it would be cold," he says, picking up the piece and stroking it with his finger. "And it's so smooth. Can you even feel anything but the temperature?"

MaryBell nods, "Good point! Some people prefer that, though. It lets you focus on one sensation at a time." She reaches over to another glass dildo, this one purple and decorated with perfectly placed bumps and ridges. "This one has texture, so you get both the coolness and some friction and pressure." She hands it to him, noticing that he touches the tip of her fingers as he takes it, running his hands up and down the shaft as he nods.

"I can see that," he agrees. "But I don't know about that glass. I think I'd be paranoid about it breaking."

"Well, I'm not going to say it's impossible because anything can happen, but these are made to take a beating, and I've never heard of anyone actually breaking one, nevermind sustaining an injury."

He puts the dildo back down on the table, fingers touching the velvet tablecloth as he does so. "Well, as you say, anything is possible."

"Yes, it is." He looks up at her words, fully meeting her gaze, and she smiles, knowing that she is flirting, knowing that it is probably a bad idea to flirt with a curious newbie, but finding herself drawn to him. Smirking a little bit, she asks, "So, is there something I can help you with?"

He laughs, a smile reaching his eyes. "Maybe." He pauses, fingers trailing along the other pieces on the table between them. "I'm looking for something...different."

"Different how?" MayBell asks, putting on her professional face.

"I'm not sure," he grins, then shakes his head. "Really helpful, I know."

"Well, let's start with the easy stuff. Is this something for you or your partner?"

This time his look is all flirtation. "I don't have a partner."

"Oh, well then. Your girlfriend then?" She tilts her head, making it clear she is joking.

He shakes his head. "Just me," he says, "and thank you for pointing out how lonely I am."

"I don't think someone like you is ever lonely," MaryBell tells him. "But are you...tired of the same old thing?"

James nods. "Exactly. If I want to try something else, what would you recommend?"

MaryBell considers him. "I think I need to know a little more about you first. Would that be okay?"

James nods.

"Let's start with your name."

"I'm James." He extends his hand to her. "And you are?"

"MaryBell," she replies, taking his hand and shaking it. It is a good grip, none of that ridiculous posturing and squeezing, but not cold and sweaty either. His touch is pleasant, and she doesn't want to let go. It has been a while since she felt such instant attraction to someone. It is refreshing. "And tell me, James," she says, flipping his hand over and examining the palm. His hand is big, but not huge, with long fingers. She feels the rough pads at the tips of his first and second finger, the classic mark of a guitar player, "Is this your first playtime or have you been here before?"

"Well, this definitely isn't my first time at the rodeo," he says, "but I've been thinking lately that I'd like to... get more involved." He lets her continue to hold his hand, watching as she runs her fingers across his palm. He looks up at her, his other hand reaching out to pick up one of her larger silicone dildos. "I want to *really* play this time."

She releases his hand and takes the toy from him. "Slow down there, cowboy. Even if this isn't your first rodeo, you'll need to ease into it." She puts back the extra-large toy and picks up a medium-sized one. She holds it up, showing him the features. "Wide base, so you don't lose it anywhere. It will actually suction cup to anything you stick it to, and it's made to fit a harness. Longer length, so it reaches the right places. A light layer of texture so you can feel some friction." At this, she takes his finger and runs it up and down the blue silicone. "And this one glows in the dark, so... bonus!"

"Does it actually glow in the dark?" he asks, curiosity mingling with surprise.

She nods. "Yep. Useful to find it, of course, but it's really cool to watch."

"So you've used this one before?"

"Well, not THAT specific one," she clarifies, then realizes that she is nearly blushing as she thinks about the last time she'd been with William. He really enjoyed that strap-on—she probably should have assumed he'd eventually decide to pursue relationships with men exclusively. "Apparently, it's pretty amazing," she pauses, then decides to just go for honesty. If James is anything like William, she'd rather know up front. "But I've heard it doesn't compare to the real thing." She waits for his reply.

"Well," James says slowly, "I think I will settle for pretty amazing then. I'm curious about the sensation, but I'm not that attracted to men, so I will pass on the real thing."

MaryBell cocks her head. "So, you are into women then?"

James nods. "Yes." It is a definite statement. MaryBell wouldn't mind if he is interested in playing with boys, but she wants him to want her as well, and she smiles at him, feeling the slow burn work its way up her neck, skin tingling as she thinks about how exciting it would be to play with a man like that again. William was a long time ago.

"Good." MaryBell pauses, debating if she is really going to do this. She isn't the type to randomly pick up a guy at an event and bring him home without getting to know him a little more first, but it has been a long time since she's been able to explore her dominant side, and James is definitely attractive. She looks him over again. He doesn't seem to be a crazed axe murderer type. *Then again, what does a crazed axe murderer look like?*

"Do you enjoy playing with toys like this?" James asks, distracting her.

MaryBell nods, "Oh yes. I love when I get the chance to use them." She pauses, then takes the plunge. "It's been a while since I've had that chance."

"Has it?" he asks, but it isn't really a question. "Huh." Now it is his turn to pause. She can practically see the thoughts spinning in his head, echoing her own. "Well, I haven't played with toys like this before, and I would love the chance to try them out."

MaryBell flushes, skin heating as she imagines him kneeling before her, hands bound and vulnerable, just begging her to fuck him. She shakes her head to clear it of the vision, deciding that she deserves this. It has been too long. But, first things first...she has bills to pay.

She points to the blue dildo in his hand. "Well, if you want to play with that toy, James, you're going to have to buy it first."

Chapter Two

Three hours later, MaryBell opens her front door to let James inside. "Hey," she says, still marveling that she has invited him back to her house after only knowing him a few hours. "You were able to find the place alright?"

"GPS got me here no problem," he replies, gesturing at his phone. "Can I park my car there?" MaryBell looks out the door at his red Nissan Sentra parked in her driveway behind her blue Mini Cooper. He is off the street, so no one will complain. Her neighbors can be a pain sometimes, but that is the price she pays for living in Hyde Park.

"Sure," she gestures for him to come inside. "But leave that phone on that table right there." She points at the side table near the front door. "No pictures. No videos."

"Of course not," James agrees, setting his phone down next to his keys. "Tonight, it's just us." She waits while he takes off his sneakers, leaving the Converse on the mat, and then his jacket, hooking it on one of the empty pegs by her front door. He pulls a package from the pocket as he hangs it up, handing the dildo to her without a word.

"Do you want anything?" she asks, taking his hand and leading him farther into the house. He takes in her simple decor, the black and white photos on the wall of the entryway, the black leather couch and Ikea TV cabinet in her living room as they make their way to her kitchen. MaryBell takes a seat across the hightop table from him, waiting as he settles onto the stool. She places the package at the edge of the table, ignoring it for the moment.

"I'm fine," he says.

"I know," she retorts, "and I can't wait to see how fine, but we need to talk about a few things first." James looks at her expectantly. "So," she begins, "let's talk about hard limits."

James smiles. "Well, like I say, this isn't my very first time, but I have limited experience. I'm not quite sure what my limits are."

MaryBell nods. "So are you okay with just telling me if I go too far? Or do you want to do the whole safe word thing?"

James shakes his head. "I'm not looking to play like that. I'm more curious about the sensation than the headspace."

"So this isn't about subspace tonight," she clarifies.

James shakes his head. "I mean, it's hot if you order me around, but it's not required. I like it, but I don't need it the entire time. You don't have to play a role or anything."

MaryBell nods again, taking his hand across the table and stroking his fingers. "Alright then. Anything else I should know about?"

James considers, face reddening as her fingers continue their slow massage. "So this is about you using that dildo on me, right?" He gestures at the package resting on the table. "How? Do you have a harness?"

MaryBell grins wickedly, letting her dominant side out a little bit. "Oh yes, cowboy. I won't just be pressing that into you with my hands. I'm going to fuck the bejesus out of you." James might not need to be submissive, but she definitely wants to dominate him.

James' quick intake of breath is encouraging, and she leans across the table, her hand caressing his face. "I'm going to grab those lovely hips, press you hard into the bed, and ride you until you scream your pleasure and beg me for more." MaryBell watches the heat rise in his neck at her words, and feels a responding pull in her lower belly. "So, James," she says in a low voice, face close to his as she puts a knee up on the tabletop and scoots over to his side, "is there anything else we should discuss before we begin? Anything I should know about?"

"Are you going to tie me up?" James' voice is breathless, his eyes tracking from hers to her lips, only a few inches from his.

"I can," she says. "Would you like that, James? Do you want me to capture you and have my way with you?"

"Yes," he replies, and this time his eyes don't leave her lips. "Will you kiss me?"

"Oh yes," she says, moving her lips to his for a soft kiss. His lips are warm and inviting, tasting of the mint gum he must have chewed on the way over to her house. He waits for her to press her tongue into his mouth, allowing her to gently run her way along his teeth before meeting her with a soft press of his own tongue. MaryBell savors the feel of him, learning the rhythm of his kiss as she brings her body around on the tabletop, shifting from knees to sitting more solidly on her backside. She lets her hands roam over his neck and back, running her fingers through his hair, caressing his ears, pressing into the muscles of his neck and back. Her legs wrap around him, and he stands suddenly, carrying her off the table and spinning her around, pressing her against the wall.

"Ooh," she whispers against his lips, feeling the hardness of his erection through his jeans. "And I thought tonight was about me dominating you a little bit."

James chuckles, deep in his chest, hands holding her ass as he presses her into the wall. "Maybe I got a little distracted," he murmurs.

"Well, I'd hate for you to miss out on your new toy," she says, running her hands through his hair as she tightens her legs around his waist, letting the wall support her. "Though I definitely want to revisit this position next time."

He raises an eyebrow, but eases back, allowing her feet to touch the floor again. "Next time, huh? That sounds promising."

"Well," she says, hands reaching for his belt and pulling him toward her, "I suppose it depends on how the rest of the evening goes, but it's shaping up quite well so far." She unbuckles his belt, undoes his button, and unzips his fly, pushing his jeans to a heap on the floor. She glances down at the considerable bulge standing proud before her. "Quite well."

He looks at her, hands running down her arms to the bottom of her dress. "Can I undress you?"

"No," she tells him. "I'm undressing you tonight." She watches the excitement on his face he releases her, biting his lip as her hands move slowly down the dress, highlighting her curves as she moves to the bottom. She lifts it over her head in a smooth motion, feeling the rush as the air hits her skin, enjoying his eyes on her body.

She thanks the gods that she had decided to wear a matching bra and panties that morning, and smiles when he takes in her blue polka dots. They aren't ultra sexy, but they are definitely cute, and considering what she is about to do to him in a little bit, she thinks cutesy is a little bit funny. His hands reach out as if to touch her, but she reaches down, grabs them, and pushes them to his hips, making him wait. Then she reaches out and pulls his shirt over his head, revealing a chest that has some lines but not too much definition. She runs her palms down his skin, feeling the hardness of muscle, but not enough to turn him into a marble statue. She lets her nails trace little lines as she touches him, enjoying the small wince as she marks him gently.

"Now," she says in a tone that allows no opposition, "come with me." She steps to the table, grabs the package, and walks back to where he stands near the door, kicking his legs free of his jeans. She waits for him to finish, then grabs his cock through his shorts and begins leading him down the short hallway to her bedroom. James doesn't resist.

Her room has the same simplicity as the rest of her house: a queen-sized four poster bed, a small night table, and a dresser. She doesn't have a TV in her bedroom, but she does have a small speaker, and she contemplates putting on some music. *No*, she decides. *I want to hear every sound he makes.*

She leads him to the edge of the bed, then releases him, steps behind him, and pushes him onto the bed. He lands on his stomach, then crawls forward onto his knees. "Not yet, cowboy," she tells him, pulling him around to face her. "I get to play with you first. Sit here."

James does as he is bid, sitting on the edge of her bed, watching as she walks over to her dresser and opens the bottom drawer. She knows he can see the gleaming toys in there. She opens the package, slowly unwrapping the layers of paper and plastic that she always uses to wrap her customers' toys. She reveals the blue dildo, runs her fingers over its smooth surface, then sets the packaging aside. She checks to make sure that James is watching—of course he is watching, eyes wide with anticipation—and then she slams the base of the dildo down onto the top of her dresser, the wide suction cup immediately sticking to the surface, the soft glow barely visible in the dim light. It sways back and forth for a second before stilling.

James chuckles from his seat on her bed. "It really does glow!"

"It glows more if you let it soak up some light all day long," she admits. "This one has only been out for a little bit, so it's not very bright. But it will be next time."

She bends down slowly to her drawer, removing a cleaning wipe, and then slowly cleans the new toy, taking time to show James just how big it is. When it is shiny, she leaves it on the dresser, leaning down again to retrieve some simple restraints. She considers her options: the wide red and black cloth straps with velcro seem the best choice for what she has in mind, though she eyes the purple bondage tape for a moment.

Nodding, she selects two of the cloth bundles, the hand ties wrapped up neatly into small circles. She ignores the matching foot restraints, knowing she won't need them tonight. She stands up, small bundles in hand, and walks over to him.

"You need to lay completely on the bed," she orders. "Head at the top, feet spread out." When James obeys, she kneels on his right side, first tying the open end of the restraint to the center of the headboard, and then wrapping the wide cloth cuff around his right wrist, making sure that the hold isn't too tight, but that the velcro securing it around the outside is definitely in place. "Give that a tug," she tells him. When James does, his arm comes to an abrupt pause at the end of the tether, and it doesn't give it all. *Nice.*

MaryBell makes a slow show of crawling across his chest, then secures his other wrist to the next post over, so James lays with both hands directly above his head. She has considered spread-eagle, but she wants him on his belly at some point, and this way she can flip him over and over, and he won't get tangled up. The ties will just slip around one another, pulling him closer to the headboard, and that is fine.

Now that she has him at her mercy, she pauses to admire his body, kneeling at his left side as she takes in the lines of chest and hip, the straining erection pressing against his boxer shorts, the way his toes keep curling and uncurling in anticipation. She runs a hand down his chest, flicking his nipples as she does so, and watches the goosebumps rise on his skin. She leans down, blowing gently on each nipple, enjoying the gasp and sigh that her breath elicits.

He watches her intently, and she keeps eye contact as she moves down his body, pausing to breathe hot air against his straining cock through the fabric. His hips raise to meet her face, his eagerness pressing himself to her. "Hey now," she chastises, and his hips fall back into the bed, allowing her to move as she would. "Let's see you," she says, then slides the waistband of his shorts down, revealing a considerable shaft. She licks the tip, swirling her tongue around the sensitive head, and when he sucks in a breath, she draws him completely into her mouth, relishing the gasp that jerks from him. She sucks gently at first, moving slowly up and down the shaft, and when his hips relax, she pulls hard, enjoying the yelp followed by a satisfied groan.

She pulls back, sliding his shorts down his legs and off. She tosses them on the floor, then turns back to her bound lover, his eyes eager and excited. She knows he is probably debating the wisdom of his decision right now. He is curious to play, sure, but right now, he is falling back on old routines, and those habits want her to climb on top and ride him to orgasm. She can understand. That cock is impressive, and having him inside of her will be delicious.

But she wants a different kind of pleasure tonight.

She slides off the bed, taking the few slow steps to her dresser, knowing that he is watching her. She bends artfully to the bottom drawer, retrieving a bottle of lube, and then she stands and grabs the dildo from the dresser top. She makes a show of lubricating the length, hands sliding all around as she walks back to the bed, sure to have enough to spread everywhere. She crawls between his legs, then gently smacks his inner thighs until he raises his knees, giving her room to kneel between his legs. She pushes his legs out, asking him to tell her where is comfortable and where is too far. Making notes of the limits of his movement, she holds the dildo with one hand, then uses her other slick hand to rub his penis again, stroking him gently at first and then a little more roughly when he seems to relax, knees falling in toward where she sits.

As she slides her hand up and down his shaft, her other hand moves toward the sweet spot below his ball sac. She waits, then presses him there suddenly, loving the gasp that escapes him. She continues her slow up and down rhythm on his cock with her hand, while reaching lower with her other hand, this time spreading his butt and revealing the prize. She spreads some lube around, then reaches for the dildo, pressing the tip against him.

He shudders, his whole body tensing up. "Relax," she tells him, keeping up the rhythm with one hand and gently pressing with the dildo. He relaxes, and the dildo creeps forward an inch or so. She presses it slowly back and forth, gaining ground with each pass, but sure to listen to his breathing and feel his muscles to see when he needs her to pause.

"How's that?" she asks, when the dildo's head disappears into his body.

"Nice," he groans.

She slows her rhythm on his cock then, knowing that too much stimulation might cause him to come right there. William did, that first time. It took three separate tries before she actually got the special Rode-oh shorts on, strapped the dildo in place, and really fucked him before he came. Apparently, the sensation is overwhelming.

She presses the dildo deeper inside, easing into him, hand holding his dick with firm pressure but no motion. He presses down into her, clearly wanting more.

"Ready, are we?" she asks in a teasing voice, then pulls the dildo completely out of him, careful to place it on the bed where it won't roll onto the floor. He moans in disappointment. "Roll over," she orders. "Hands and knees."

As he obeys, she crosses to the dresser once more. She slides her polka dot panties off, replacing them with the pair of special shorts, and slides them up her hips, relishing the feel of the tight material pressing against her skin. She steps to the bed, knowing that James must be wondering what she is doing, enjoying the anticipation as it builds. She picks up the dildo, and slides it through the small circle cut into the front of the shorts. She presses it firmly into the ring of fabric meant to hold it in place, then presses it back against her, feeling the pressure against her clit.

This is going to be so awesome.

She considers adding the vibrator to the small pouch inside the special panties, but decides against it. She wants to feel herself pressing into him each thrust. Vibration would help her come faster, sure, but she doesn't need the encouragement tonight. She is burning.

She picks up the lube again, running a bead along the length of the dildo one more time before she climbs on to the bed behind James. She presses against his legs until his knees are about shoulder width apart, then presses the tip of the dildo against his exposed flesh.

"Are you okay?" she asks, unable to read his expression because his face is pressed into the bed.

"Yes," he grunts. "So more than okay."

"Good," she tells him. "Now tell me if it's too much. I will stop."

"Okay," he mumbles into the mattress, and then she feels him readjust his head, likely resting his forehead on top of his bound hands.

"Good boy," she says, unable to resist. She presses the dildo against him again, insistent this time, and then reaches around his hip with her right hand to rub his penis again. He is too large for her to easily reach the entire shaft, but she can reach enough to feel the hardness, the eagerness in him. She rubs him in a slow but determined rhythm, and then pushes the dildo inside him, just a little bit. He groans, and then tenses up. She waits, hand still stroking his cock, and he relaxes again. She pushes into him slowly, inch by inch, pausing as he needs, listening to his body, trying to ignore the slow burn of her own that grows each time she presses into him, the wide base of the dildo pressing hard against her clit. She wants to shove into him and start bouncing, rubbing herself against that hard surface, but she forces herself to wait, enjoying the slow temptation as she works inside him.

Soon enough, the dildo makes it beyond that place deep within him. She feels the ease of friction, and his whole body spasms against her. She thinks he has come, unable to help himself, but he moans, pressing his ass against her hips and gently wiggling back and forth, wanting more. She can feel the warmth of pre-cum on his dick, and she knows he won't last much longer.

But this is the fun part.

"You okay?"

"Mmm-hmm."

"Good." Without any warning, she withdraws and pushes back into him, pressing the length of the dildo deep inside, slipping past that sweet spot that elicits another moan.

When he doesn't tighten up, but presses himself harder against her, she pulls back and dives in again, loving the pressure against her clit, feeling her own pleasure building, building.

"Oh fuck yes!" James yells as she draws back again.

"You like that, cowboy?" MaryBell asks, releasing his cock to place both hands on his hips, and yanks him back against her, relishing the pressure against her clit, that sweet feeling growing in her belly. "You like it when I fuck you?" She punctuates each word with another thrust, feeling his body buck in wild abandon. She is close now, so close, her hands digging into his hips with each push and pull.

"Oh yes!" he cries, and his whole body tenses up, orgasm flooding him. MaryBell thrusts into him two more times, her own orgasm wracking her body as she presses hard into him that last time. She collapses onto his back, pulse pounding in her fingertips, her hands still gripping his hips as if they are the only thing tethering her to the world.

For a moment, she is sure she will just float away if she lets go, but then the feeling passes, and she sits up, easing out of him as she backs away. She leaves him kneeling for a moment, letting him gather himself as she slips off the bed and out of the shorts. She places them in a pile on top of the dresser, knowing she will clean up later on.

James rolls slowly over, hands still bound over his head, face red with exertion, breathing heavily from his release.

"So," MaryBell says in her best customer service, "are you satisfied with your purchase tonight, James?"

James only moans in response.

Chapter Three

MaryBell sits in her car, wondering again why she has agreed to this. Just one date, James said. It will be fun, he cajoled, like dressing up and pretending to be a normal couple. She stares out the windshield at the sign at the edge of the parking lot: The Columbia. Of course, there is hardly anything more routine than a dinner date at the fanciest restaurant in Ybor City. The only way he could be more traditional would be if he'd taken her for steak at Bern's. By choosing The Columbia, he is being "different" and "exotic" in that way that all of these vanilla boys always think will excite the girls they pick up at the bar.

But they didn't meet at the bar. They met at a fetish club, and she came to terms with her sexuality a long time ago. It feels like a betrayal of sorts, to agree to come here and pretend to go on a "normal" date when all she really wants is to grab his hips and yank him back against her strap-on, feeling him tighten and hearing him moan in ways that she doesn't think any of those vanilla boys ever do during sex. She grins at the memory, unable to help herself. For a new boy toy, James is turning out to be way more fun than she anticipated. Even with ridiculous dinner dates, she knows that her playtime with him is only getting started.

She gives herself one more look in the rear view mirror before getting out of the car. She can play vanilla for a little while. Besides, she is always a sucker for good food.

The brief walk across the parking lot gives her a chance to adjust her dress, the baby blue material silky against her skin as she makes sure the back isn't riding up. She pulled out some lingerie for tonight, her garters buckled to the stockings at her thighs, her feet tucked into cute but comfortable low heels. If the wind doesn't gust, she shouldn't end up pulling a Marilyn Monroe on her way inside the restaurant. The air is humid, as always in Florida, but not the oppressive heat she knows is coming soon. She is trying hard to enjoy these last few days of relative coolness, imprinting the feeling in her memory to keep her steady during the sweat-soaked months ahead.

James already waits for her inside, looking sharp in his khakis and a button down shirt. He gives a little wave when he sees her, offering his arm as they approach the hostess.

Dinner is pleasant enough, filled with small getting-to-know-you topics like favorites and pastimes, past jobs and future plans, subtle and not-so-subtle flirtation, limits hard and soft, known and unknown, fingers touching on the table and some adventurous foot exploration under the table. MaryBell is glad that the tables have tablecloths, her stockinged feet completely hidden as she presses and rubs against James' crotch. When the server asks if they want dessert, she almost says yes, if only to prolong James' torture, but her belly is filled with delicious spiced meats and rice, and she doesn't want to eat anything else, especially knowing that the rest of the evening will likely be filled with vigorous activity.

They take a walk afterward, enjoying Ybor City at night, that magic hour right after the normal daytime shops have closed, but before the drunks and crazies really start living it up in the bars and clubs that line 7th Avenue. She points to the pizza shop across from the Ritz. "That place has the best pizza in Tampa," she declares. "Hands down."

He gestures at the cigar shop a few doors down. "This place has the best cigars in Tampa," he counters. "Hands down."

MaryBell looks at him. "You smoke?"

He shrugs. "Every now and then. I enjoy a good cigar with a whiskey." At her look, he adds, "Hey, I can be a stereotypical male sometimes."

"Not often," she comments, swatting his ass as they continue down the street.

"No," he agrees. "But I enjoy sensations. I want to try as many as I can."

When they reach the corner, he turns left, taking her hand as they walk slowly around the block and back in the direction of the parking lot where her car waits. It is quiet, the sun slowly disappearing behind the buildings, the everblue sky darkening to indigo when he pauses, steps closer to her, slowly easing them off the center of the sidewalk and over to the brick wall of the building. He presses against her, hands holding hers at her sides, looking at her with that slow smile, and then he kisses her, soft at first, but quickly building to something harder and more fierce. He pulls her wrists together in front of her body, holds them both with one hand, and then uses the other to rake through her hair, pulling the long dark tresses down from her perfectly messy bun.

MaryBell moans against his lips. When they pause for breath, she whispers, "I was hoping you would pin me up against a wall again, James."

"I'm glad to oblige," James replies, his hands leaving her hair to push both of her hands up above her head and against the wall. His hips press into her, and she braces her body weight on her left leg, lifting her right leg up to hook around him. His hands leave hers, roaming free over her shoulders, waist, and around the swell of her bottom. She feels him pause as he feels the hard line of the garter running down her thigh, and he breaks the kiss. "You came prepared."

"Always," she breathes. She wants more, to keep kissing him, rubbing against him, but they are standing outside in the street. Anyone could be watching.

The thought only excites her more.

She gives a furtive look around in the growing twilight. It isn't late enough for anyone to have stumbled onto 6th Avenue yet. People walking here will have a specific destination. MaryBell doesn't see anyone. She gives James a delightfully wicked look, and then glances again from side to side.

No one walks. No cars move on the brick-lined street. There are a few cars parked on the street, but no one seems in a hurry to get into them. They are fairly hidden against the wall, standing as they are underneath an overhang, tucked between two doors that are probably employee exits. She doesn't see any telltale cigarette butts near the doors though; it is unlikely that any employees would come bursting outside for a smoke break.

James makes the same surveillance, hands never leaving her body, feeling her butt through the silky material of her dress, then skirting beneath to caress her bare skin. "Naughty girl," he murmurs, deft fingers stroking the damp center between her legs. She presses closer to him, her leg wrapping hard around his lower leg, trying to not be so incredibly obvious if someone does happen to walk by. His hand continues to press, fingers moving slowly back and forth, building the heat within her. When she moans, he kisses her, swallowing the sound as he moves his lips in concert with his fingers. She can feel the press of his erection, but at the moment, she doesn't care. All that matters are those fingers pressing, rubbing, caressing, and his mouth on hers.

"Yes," she says into his mouth, "dear god James like that yes!"

As the orgasm spills through her, her muscles lock, the rushing wave paralyzing her, and then she sags, boneless, and James holds her upright as she shudders with the force of her release.

When she thinks she can stand without difficulty, MaryBell puts her foot down and leans against the wall. James pulls away, face suffused with pleasure. "That was fun," he says, offering her his hand as he steps back, glancing quickly up and down the street, noting again that they are still alone. "I've always wanted to do that."

"What? Make out on 6th Avenue?" MaryBell is still a little breathless, but she takes his hand and starts slowly down the street back to the parking lot.

"Well, sure, but really, I always wanted to make a woman come in public, not sure if we would get caught." He pauses, grinning at her, then pulls her hand up to his lips and kisses it. "And thank you, MaryBell, for being so prepared."

"There is something to be said for old school lingerie," she admits, "but I always find panties to be a nuisance."

He nods, and they continue walking, both of them glowing with satisfaction of a night well begun, but not yet finished, each knowing that even more pleasures awaits.

Chapter Four

MaryBell follows James to his condo in one of the high rise buildings on Channelside, leaving her car in the visitor spot when he parks in his assigned space. He walks with her through the well-lit garage to the elevator, holding hands as they wait for it to arrive. When they step inside, MaryBell looks at the numbers on the panel. "What floor?"

"20." He taps the button, and the elevator begins to rise smoothly.

"Is that the penthouse?" she asks, smiling at him.

"No," he says, pulling her to him for a kiss. "Are you sorry I'm not that kind of guy?"

MaryBell returns the kiss, feeling the heat begin to build in her belly again. "No," she says. "I like you as you are, James. I don't need a penthouse to make me like you more." She kisses him again, then pulls away to laugh, "Of course, on the 20th floor, I'm expecting an amazing view."

"That I do have," he replies, hands tugging at her hair. "I have a balcony, too, and I can't wait to have you out there, bare ass naked, pressed against the railing, all of this glorious hair blowing free in the wind."

MaryBell moans, arms reaching around him, hands tugging his shirt out of his pants so her fingers can skate up his back and rake him with her nails. The elevator arrives, and they pull apart, stepping out into a short hallway done in neutral beige. There is a table with fresh flowers in a vase set across from the elevator.

Noticing MaryBell's curious glance at the flowers, James says, "It's the condo association. They maintain the hallways, deal with the garbage, and make sure every floor has fresh flowers. You know, the important things."

"Do you get room service, too?" MaryBell jokes.

James grins. "Not quite, but there are quite a few places who deliver here." He assumes a serious air. "You do know that Channelside is *the* up and coming neighborhood in Tampa, of course?"

"Of course," she replies in the same tone, "and the view from that balcony better be amazing for the price of this 'up and coming' neighborhood. I remember when the only thing here was the arena and the aquarium."

"Me too. I was lucky enough to get in at the start, back when there were only a few buildings and a lot of hope and promises."

"Nicely done," she compliments him as they approach his doorway. "Are you always so good at spying an opening?"

James turns to grin at her as he turns the key in his front door with a look that is all male. "Sometimes."

MaryBell smiles back at him, then pushes him into the condo as the door opens. He turns to face her, using his momentum to drag her in behind him, foot kicking the door shut behind them. "Now," he tells her, "it's my turn."

MaryBell shivers in anticipation, then pauses to consider the entryway. "Do I get a tour first?" she asks in a low innocent voice.

"But of course," James replies, "but I won't lead you around by your dick."

"That's only because I didn't bring my toys tonight."

"No worries. I have some of my own." He waves for her to follow. "Welcome to my lovely home," he grins, leading her into the open plan living room and kitchen. "Bathroom behind you," he points to a door in the wall behind her, "but the bigger one is off the master." He gestures at the glass doors on the far side of the room, "The fabled balcony which you will certainly see later." He leads her down a small hallway off to the right, "Bedroom is right here." MaryBell glances inside to see a bed with a metal headboard, but he doesn't go in. "And this is my office." He steps inside, and MaryBell follows, taking in the desk and chair, but completely impressed by the wall of windows overlooking the Hillsborough River and the port.

She walks over to the windows, placing a hand against the cool glass, "You work from home?"

James walks up behind her. "Yup," he says, kissing her neck and pulling at the tie that holds her hair in place. She fixed the bun during the short drive over here, but she knows it is a lost cause. He tugs it free, and her hair spills down her back. "Finally," he breathes. "I've wanted to do that since we first met."

"Play with my hair?" she asks, pressing her hips back against him. "Is that what you've been longing for, James?"

He spins her around to face him. "Among other things, but I think we've already played with walls tonight." He takes her hand, and then motions for her to sit in the desk chair. It is surprisingly comfortable, she notes, with perfect lower back support and a high back for her head to lean against.

"This is a nice chair," she observes, hands pressing into the armrests.

"It better be," he says. "I spend a lot of my time sitting in it." He pauses, and then reaches into a small bin tucked underneath the desk.

"And the next time I do, I want to think of you sitting in it." He reaches into the bin, pulling out black restraints, a wide cuff with velcro on the outside attached to a long strap meant to be tied to anything. "Now," he orders, in a tone that sends thrills through her belly, "take off your dress."

MaryBell scoots the silky material out from under her butt, and then slips it over her head, tossing it on top of the closed laptop that rests on the desk. She leans back into the chair, spreading her legs, stockings and garters matching the simple pattern of her bra. She looks down at herself. "Anything else," she pauses, then adds, "Master?"

He chuckles, but seems to consider. He idly flips the restraints against one palm as he stands. "Your bra," he says. "How much do you like it?"

Now it is MaryBell's turn to consider him. "Why do you ask?"

He reaches for her hand, and she gives it to him, face curious. He secures the cuff around her wrist, making sure the velcro is tight but not uncomfortable. "How's that?" He lets her ponder as he cuffs the other wrist. With the restraints around both wrists, MaryBell takes a moment to touch each one with her still mobile hands, checking the tension against her skin. Finding it bearable, she nods, and then James yanks on the ends of the restraints, first lifting her hands out in front of her with a grin, then tugging them down and to her sides as he spreads his arms wide. Standing up, he moves around behind the chair, keeping the tension on the straps as he secures them, tucking her hands next to her waist, firm against the back of the chair.

"Is this a favorite bra?" he asks again from behind her now, giving her some slack in the ties, but only enough to rest her hands next to her butt. It isn't tight enough to pull her shoulders oddly though. She is quite comfortable.

"No," she admits, speaking over her shoulder to where he kneels, securing the straps. "It's pretty generic, to be honest. I got the beige to match the garter, really, and those I do love."

"Noted," James says, standing up behind her and spinning the chair to face him. "So," he begins in a low voice, one hand reaching behind the chair to grab something off the desk, "you wouldn't mind if I," he pauses, pulling the pair of scissors in front of her, "cut it off?"

MaryBell gapes at him. They discussed limits over dinner, but this hasn't come up. She considers it, deciding that the very idea of him cutting her bra off her while she sits tied to his chair is thrilling. "No," she tells him, "I wouldn't mind."

"Good," he says, pressing the scissors under one strap. The cool metal makes her shiver, and then he snips the material. The strap falls down, and gravity goes to work almost immediately. MaryBell has large breasts, and without the support, her right breast relaxes. She looks down at it, and then at him. He reaches out, pushes the cup underneath to free her skin, and puts his mouth on her nipple. MaryBell sighs at the warm rush of his lips. His hands hold her waist, then run down her legs, tracing the line of the garters from her hips to her thighs. He keeps his mouth on her nipple, sucking harder and then softer, alternating rhythm, and she wants to press his head against her. She reaches out, but her hands stop at the end of the restraints, fingers straining uselessly against her sides. He releases her nipple, and then retrieves the scissors from where he has abandoned them on the floor. He runs the cool metal across the sensitive skin of her collarbone, and then snips the other strap. Her bra folds down, but instead of tucking it under as he has her first breast, he uses the scissors once more in the middle, then pushes the bra aside, hands caressing her bare skin.

James kisses her breasts, then scoots down, rolling the chair closer to where he kneels, and pushes her back into a reclined position. The chair leans back in that terrifying way for a moment, and MaryBell gasps, but then she hears a click as the chair locks into position, and she relaxes, looking down her body at James' dark head now poised above her middle.

He looks up at her, eyes dark with anticipation. "You want me to touch you?"

MaryBell nods, straining to raise her body to meet him, but her hands keep her tethered to the chair.

James traces a line down her belly, then runs his hand between her legs and slips into her wetness. "You want me here?" His fingers are quick, rubbing against her clit in the way he knows she likes.

"Yes," she moans.

James slips a finger down, sliding inside of her. MaryBell strains harder, trying to press her hips against him. "You like me inside you?"

"God yes!" she says, as he begins to move his finger in and out in a teasing rhythm. James uses his free hand to lift one leg over his shoulder and then the other, and then bends to lick her, tongue warm and demanding against her secret flesh, his other hand never pausing in the rhythm. James knows his business, and the combination of sucking and licking with his finger inside has her shuddering within moments. She longs for her hands, wanting to press his head into her body, wanting the feeling to never stop, and then the wave rushes over her, and she quivers in the chair, body going limp as the orgasm crests and then fades. James lifts his head, resting his cheek against her thigh. "I love how you look right after you come."

MaryBell focuses on catching her breath, enjoying the support of the chair as she floats back down from the euphoria of the orgasm. James moves away from her, lifts the chair upright, and spins her so he kneels behind her. She feels him untie the restraints, and then he spins the chair again, pulling the ties around in front of her, and then he stands up, tugging her after him, using the restraints as a guide. "I believe I promised you a lovely view," he says, leading her out of the room on shaky legs. She follows, and when James opens the balcony door, she shivers as the cool air brushes her naked skin.

The balcony runs the length of the room, but MaryBell sees that James only has a table and one chair outside. She looks out into the night sky, realizing that she can see the boats in the port across the river, but it is unlikely that anyone could see them up here, since they are so high off the ground. She looks at the chest high railing and then at James, eyebrow quirked.

"It's sturdy," he says. "Trust me."

"I do," she says, watching as he lets go of her restraints long enough to remove his shirt and kick off his pants. His erection is a huge bulge in his boxers, and MaryBell's belly tingles, eager to feel him inside of her. "So," she says, standing before him in only her garters and stockings, hands cuffed, but the tethers trailing on the floor in front of her. "Where do you want me?"

James walks toward her, picking up the restraints and using them to pull her closer to him. "Well, I think I want you outside on the balcony, all that glorious hair running riot down your back while I fuck you from behind..." He pauses, then grins. "But I want to see your face this time, so maybe we'll keep that for later."

MaryBell feels an answering smile on her own face. "So...?"

He gestures at the table. "Hop up."

She does, gasping as the cold table top hits her bare skin, spreading her legs where she perches on the edge. James steps out of his shorts, his cock hard in the moonlight as he puts the condom on, and MaryBell reaches a hand to touch him, only to have James use the restraints to pull her hand away.

"Oh no," he tells her with a playful smirk. "Tonight is my night to play."

MaryBell puts both hands down at her sides, smiling innocently at him. "I only want..." she lets the words trail off, wanting to keep the game going.

"I know what you want," he says, stepping right in front of her, cock pressed against her opening, but gentle, so gentle. She longs to scoot forward, to feel all of that hard length inside of her, but she stops herself. "You want to pull me into you, want to ride my cock, want to come again and again."

"Well, yes," she admits, skin flushed with anticipation as the tip of his cock teases her, presses hard against her but does not move. "I do want to do that, but right now, I just want you to fuck me."

His hands find the restraints, wrapping the tethers around and tugging her hands behind her back while moving her toward him a fraction of an inch, and all that hardness is touching her now, her skin aching for him to move, to push into her, but he holds himself firm. "Look at me," he urges, and she tilts her head back, eyes looking into his as he wraps one arm around her back and the other grabs her hip. She can feel the restraints pressing into her skin as he pulls her hands tighter behind her back, but it is a delicious feeling. If her hands were free, she would be climbing him by now, forcing her pleasure even while he wanted to linger in the moment. His cock moves another fraction closer, and she feels her skin pull around him as he stretches her. She aches for more, her whole body trying to press into him.

"Wait for it," he tells her, eyes never leaving hers as he creeps inside of her. "You naughty little vixen," he purrs, giving her another small motion. He is inside of her now, but barely, just the tip, her skin screaming for more. "You need to learn some patience," he says, smiling as he gives her yet another inch. "You spend so much time ordering people around, having your way with them when you want it, as you want it," and here he pulls out a little bit, eliciting a moan of frustration from MaryBell. She squirms, trying to get that precious inch back, but he holds her tight. "You need to learn to slow down," he urges, and then he moves forward again, teasing her with his cock slowly, each movement a torrent of tortured delight. She groans when he makes it halfway, relishing in the fullness of him, sensitive skin thrilling at each slight movement. She closes her eyes then, bites her lip, and looks at him with pleading eyes.

"Please," she begs. "Please fuck me."

James gives her another inch, and then pauses. "I am fucking you," he tells her.

"More," she moans. "I need more."

"Do you?" he asks, and then with a swift moment, he sheaths himself to the core. MaryBell screams with the sudden ferocity, and her head falls back. But then James' hand is in her hair, yanking her face back up to see his. He draws back and plunges into her again, and MaryBell's body shivers, the combination of sensation and the cool air almost sending her right over the edge into another orgasm. "Yes!" she yells, and then James' mouth is on hers, tongue demanding as he moves against her again, body hard as he fills her. MaryBell wraps her legs around his hips, urging him on to greater speeds, and almost immediately, he stops moving, cock barely inside of her. She opens eyes that she hasn't realized she has closed to look at him.

"Oh no," he tells her. "You don't get to set the rhythm this time." He waits, then plunges in and out of her, hovering just outside. "This time," and he begins the long, slow push inside again, "you are at my mercy."

MaryBell lets her legs fall from his hips, willing herself not to move, relishing the feel of him pressing into her with long, slow strokes. She can feel her orgasm building, knows that if he moves just like that for a few more seconds, she will come, the wave crashing over her in a daze.

"Please," she whispers against his mouth, loving how his hand tangles itself in her hair at the base of her neck, his other hand pressed tight against her hip with the restraints pulled taut across her lower back.

He pulls away just enough to see her face. "Please what?"

"Please fuck me," she pauses a moment, then adds, "Master."

He moves faster into her at the word, hips pressing hard. "What was that?" he asks, though he has clearly heard her.

"Please fuck me, Master!" she yells, and he buries his head in her neck, mouth sucking at the skin above her collarbone as he begins to pound into her in earnest. The table begins to rock dangerously, and he lifts her, abandoning the restraints so the straps fall free. Her legs wrap hard against him as he spins, pressing her against the concrete wall next to the balcony doors and fucking her with such force that she begins to come almost immediately. She slides her hands around his neck, restraints forgotten in the sudden passion, and kisses him, reveling in the total wild abandon of the moment. She cries out her pleasure, biting James' shoulder in her excitement, and he drives himself into her two more times before his body shudders. He holds her up for another moment, both of them breathing heavily, and then his arms shake alarmingly, and they both slide down the wall, her legs releasing his waist as they sit on the balcony floor.

MaryBell laughs breathlessly. "And I thought you said we were done with walls for one night."

James shrugs, chest heaving as he catches his breath, then reaches for her wrists to release the restraints. "I guess I got excited."

MaryBell catches his face with her newly freed hand. "I like it when you get excited." She leans forward to kiss him, this time slow and gentle, a kiss just for fun, not leading anywhere.

When they separate, James finds his feet and stands up, then offers his hand to lift her up. They go back inside, James wandering into the kitchen and opening the fridge. He comes back to hand her a bottle of water.

She takes it gratefully, taking a swig and sighing. "So, James," she says, "are we going to do this again sometime?"

"I hope so," he says. "I expect you to bring your strap-on."

ALI WHIPPE

*A*li Whippe is the pen name of a professor in the higher education system who delights in imagining naughty distractions while enduring endless mind-numbing committee meetings. She loves to push the boundaries of the written word and the imagination, knowing that life at work would be way more exciting if more people didn't wear panties.

MORE BOOKS BY ALI WHIPPE

Office Hours
Tutoring Center
Athletics
Extra Credit
Bound for Release
Fetish Circuit

4 Horsemen Publications

Erotica

Dalia Lance
My Home on Whore Island
Slumming It on Slut Street
Training of the Tramp
72% Match
It Was Meant To Be... Or Whatever

Chastity Veldt
Molly in Milwaukee
Irene in Indianapolis
Lydia in Louisville
Natasha in Nashville

Honey Cummings
Sleeping with Sasquatch
Cuddling with Chupacabra
Naked with New Jersey Devil
Laying with the Lady in Blue
Wanton Woman in White
Beating it with Bloody Mary

Beau and Professor Bestialora
The Goat's Gruff
Goldie and Her Three Beards
Pied Piper's Pipe
Princess Pea's Bed

LGBT Erotica

Grayson Ace
How I Got Here
First Year Out of the Closet
You're Only a Top?
You're Only a Bottom?
I Think I'm a Serial Swiper

Leo Sparx
Claiming Alexander
Taming Alexander
Saving Alexander

4HorsemenPublications.com